BABAR
AND THE GHOST

GHOST

LAURENT DE BRUNHOFF

Abrams Books for Young Readers, New York

One beautiful day, King Babar and Queen Celeste took their children—Pom, Flora, and Alexander—and Cousin Arthur, Cornelius, and the Old Lady on a hike to the Black Castle.

But when they reached the castle, the weather changed.
"Let's go inside and get out of the rain," Arthur said.

"That's a terrible idea!" replied Cornelius. "The castle could be haunted."

Babar laughed. "Let's go inside. There is no such thing as a ghost."

When they entered the castle, Arthur saw a white shape floating at the end of a hallway. It came and went so fast that he wondered if he had really seen it.

Babar built a fire in the living room fireplace to help everyone dry off.

Arthur said nothing about the white shape. Babar had said there was no such thing as a ghost.

It was still raining, so Babar and Celeste decided they
should spend the night in the castle.
   "Great!" shouted the children. "Now we can explore!"

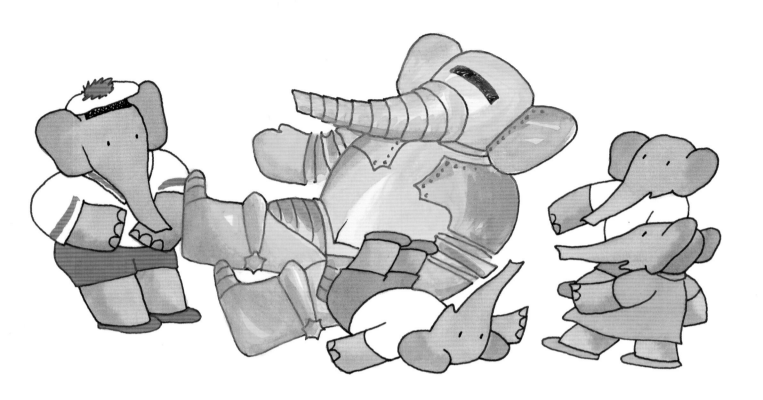

As they chased each other, they bumped into a heavy suit
of armor and knocked it over. The suit of armor sat up!
A ghost poked its head out of the helmet. *A real ghost!*

Without a sound, the ghost rose out of the suit of armor.

Terrified, the children fled up the staircase.

They ran to Babar and Celeste and told them about the ghost.

"I warned you this castle might be haunted!" said Cornelius.

"There is no such thing as a ghost," Babar reassured them. "Let's all sleep in this room, and we'll go back to Celesteville in the morning."

The adults fell asleep, but the children were wide awake.
   "Why don't we try to find the ghost again," said Arthur.
   "Let's go!" said Flora.
   They all crept silently into the hallway.

The children wandered from room to room. Suddenly they heard a voice behind them.

"Good evening. I am Baron Bardula." It was the ghost!

"This is a painting of me when I was a knight, a long time ago."

He disappeared for a moment and then came back through the wall!

The baron was a friendly ghost. He showed the children around the castle and told them of his battles and adventures.

Pom said, "Come back with us to Celesteville!"

"That could be fun," Bardula said with a little smile. "It gets lonely here."

Early the next morning, they all started back
to Celesteville. Babar, Celeste, Cornelius,
and the Old Lady did not realize that a ghost
was with them.

Back in Celesteville, everyone was curious about where they had been.
   Arthur ran to his friend Zephir the monkey and said, "Just wait until you hear what we brought back with us!"

Arthur told Zephir all about the ghost. "Only we can see him! What fun we can have!" he said. And indeed, funny things started to happen immediately.

A lemonade pitcher rose into the air on its own.

And a lawn mower ran all by itself, right through the flowers!

Cornelius was reading in the study when he felt someone snatch off his eyeglasses. He dropped his book and jumped in surprise. "Someone stole my glasses!" he complained to Babar.

After dinner, when Babar and Celeste played music with
Arthur and the Old Lady, the saxophone started squawking.
    "How did that happen?" asked Babar. Arthur laughed
because he knew the ghost was trying to play.

The next day, the ghost had a good time in the park with Alexander and Zephir. Nobody except the children understood what was happening.

Hide-and-seek was the ghost's favorite game. The children chased after him, knocking over chairs. They finally found him in a drawer, folded like a sheet. They laughed and laughed.

The door flew open. "What's all this racket?" asked Babar.

In no time at all, out in the street, horns began honking, tires screeched, and everyone started shouting.

A blue car was racing through traffic—without a driver!

The police—along with Babar, Zephir, and Arthur—went after
the driverless car, but it outran them. Then Babar received
a call informing him that the children at the elementary school
were out of control.

"They are pretending to play with a ghost!" said the principal.

Babar frowned. "Let's hurry to the school," he said, "and find
out what's going on."

On the playground the children were shouting, "The ghost! There's the ghost!" Babar saw no ghost, but he took no chances.

"Ghost," he said, "I don't believe in you, but if you are there, listen. You are turning everything topsy-turvy in Celesteville. Please leave us alone."

His plea touched the ghost. That evening, Baron Bardula told the children that he was going home. "I had a wonderful time," he said, "but it's time to go."

The children waved good-bye and begged him to visit. "I will, my friends!" he said as he faded into the night sky.

The artwork for each picture is prepared using watercolor on paper.
This text is set in 16-point Comic Sans. Hand lettering by Beata Szpura.

The Library of Congress has cataloged the original Abrams edition of this book as follows:

Library of Congress Cataloging-in-Publication Data

Brunhoff, Laurent de.
     Babar and the ghost / Laurent de Brunhoff.
          p. cm.
Summary: The friendly ghost of the Black Castle follows Babar the elephant, along with
his family and friends, back to Celesteville to spend some time with them.
     ISBN 0-8109-4398-0
     [1. Elephants—Fiction. 2. Ghosts—Fiction.] I. Title.

PZ7.B82843 Baag 2001
[E]—dc21   00-051082

ISBN for this edition: 978-1-4197-0380-5

Printed and bound in China
10 9 8 7 6 5 4 3 2

Abrams Books for Young Readers are available at special discounts when purchased in quantity
for premiums and promotions as well as fundraising or educational use. Special editions can
also be created to specification. For details, contact specialsales@abramsbooks.com or
the address below.

115 West 18th Street
New York, NY 10011
www.abramsbooks.com